Happy Birthday

to

HALEY

Good Books™

Intercourse, PA 17534
800/762-7171 • www.goodbks.com

I061686-4

Text by Lois Rock
Illustrations copyright © 2002 Gabriella Buckingham
Original edition published in English under the title
Now You Are 4 by Lion Publishing, plc, Oxford, England.
Copyright © Lion Publishing 2002.

North American edition published by Good Books, 2002.
All rights reserved.

NOW YOU ARE 4
Copyright © 2002 by Good Books, Intercourse, PA 17534
International Standard Book Number: 1-56148-397-4
Library of Congress Catalog Card Number: 2002024121

Printed and bound in Singapore.

Library of Congress Cataloging-in-Publication Data
Rock, Lois
  Now you are 4 / Lois Rock, Gabriella Buckingham.
    p. cm.
  Originally published: Oxford, England : Lion Pub., 2002.
  Summary: Four-year-olds spend their birthdays drawing, dreaming, making
friends, cutting cake, and playing.
  ISBN 1-56148-397-4
  [1. Birthdays--Fiction. 2. Stories in rhyme.] I. Title: Now you are four.
II. Buckingham, Gabriella. III. Title.
PZ8.3.R58615 No 2002
[E]--dc21   2002024121

First you were a baby,
then you grew some more...

Last year you were quite grown-up, and this year

you are

4

Here's a birthday
message from
the golden shining sun:
welcome to another year
of happiness and fun.

You can go out
and about in the world,
you can go out
and explore

the whole wide world
that is waiting out there
to welcome you
now you are 4.

July

August

September

October

November

December

30 days hath September,
April, June and November.
All the rest have 31
excepting February alone,
which has 28 days clear
and 29 in each leap year.

One line draws a wiggly thing,
two lines mark a kiss.

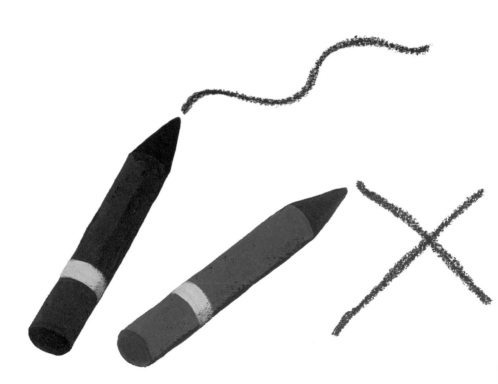

Three lines make a triangle –
and four, a shape like this!

When you are four
you can sit by yourself
and dream a whole hour away.

When you are four
you can make lots of friends:
together you all can play.

When you have to cut a cake
for everyone to share,
cut it very carefully
so every slice is fair.

Time for **noisy**

time for hush

time for *slowly*

time for **rush...**

Time for **muddy**

time for clean

The angel of dreams
is dressed in blue –
a dream for me
and a dream for you...

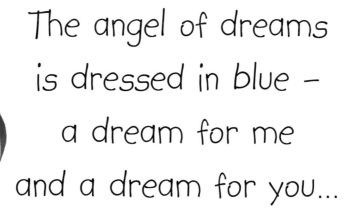

The angel of dreams
is dressed in pink –
and softly into
your bed you sink.

The angel of dreams
is dressed in white –

the day is done
and so goodnight.